GIANT

Juliet & Charles Snape

Julia MacRae Books

A division of Walker Books

Copyright © 1989 Juliet & Charles Snape
All rights reserved
First published in Great Britain 1989
by Julia MacRae Books
A division of Walker Books Ltd
87 Vauxhall Walk
London SE11 5HJ

Printed in Singapore by Tien Wah Press (Pte.) Ltd.

British Library Cataloguing in Publication Data

Snape, Juliet
  Giant.
  I. Title II. Snape, Charles
  823'.914[J]

  ISBN 0-86203-360-8

Lia and her family lived in a village at the foot of a mountain.

The villagers called their mountain "Giant".
For many years they had used Giant.

Giant's plants gave them fruit. The village
animals grazed on her slopes.

The villagers picnicked in shady places
and played in the trees.

Lia and her brother, Felix, often spent whole days
on the mountain. All the children played there.

One night Giant awoke. She looked down at her coat. Then after a while she said, "They have not cared for me. I will go away."

While the village slept, Giant rose and strode
off towards the sea.

Lia woke up
Something was wrong. She ran outside.
"Giant's gone!" she cried.
People ran to look. It was true.

"Whatever shall we do?" asked the villagers.
"Where will our sheep graze?" cried one.
"We will have no fruit!" wailed another.
"Where will we play?" moaned the children.

"We can fill the hole!" said one of the villagers,
"and build a new mountain."
"Yes," said another. The villagers set about the task,
using anything they could find.

Lia saw Giant from the top of the new plastic and metal mountain.

"Oh!" cried Lia, "she seems so sad. Why didn't we look after her?"
"We don't need her any more," replied the villagers.

But as time passed the people of the village became
worried. Nothing would grow on the new mountain.
"It's ugly," said Lia.
"And it smells," said Felix.
"Why don't we burn it down?" said the villagers.

Soon the new mountain was on fire.

The plastic and metal mountain turned into a blazing mountain of fire.

Thick black smoke blotted out the sun and everything
in the village became dark.
The villagers were afraid.

Lia ran down to the beach.
She called to Giant, "Help us please! We need you!"
Soon all the people of the village had joined Lia.
They pleaded with Giant to save them.

Giant came to the edge of the water. Lia stepped forward.
"We are sorry," she said.
"Please come back," shouted the villagers.

I have been lonely, thought Giant. She stood up and strode
back to the village.
She pulled up the river bed and poured water on the fire.
With an enormous breath, Giant blew away the black
smoke. The people cheered..

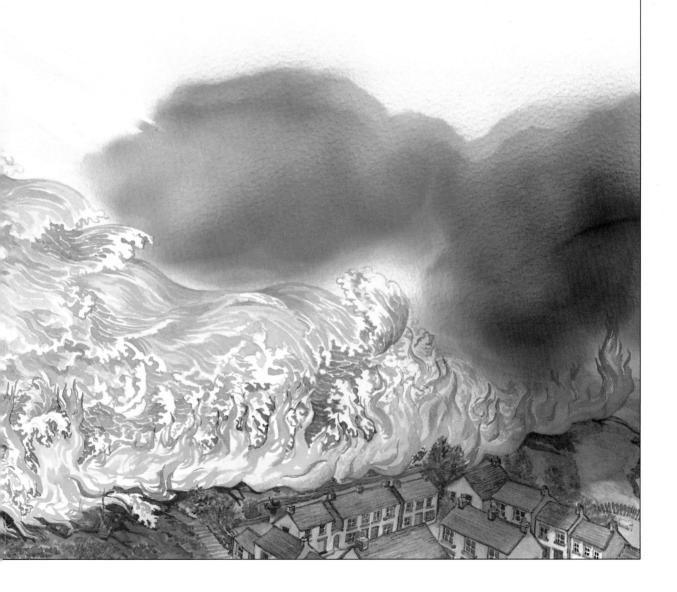

The villagers would not take their mountain for granted again.